Reverse E

Flemming George

abuddhapress@yahoo.com

ISBN: 9798880151448

Flemming George 2024

®™©

Alien Buddha Press 2024

Contents

A Stereo Shift	6
Static Surround	7
Slow Drift	9
Limits of Control	12
On the Sofa	13
Cutback	15
Normalization/ Dehumanization	17
In the Glasshouse	18
Hang Ten	19
From a London Bus	20
Broken Record	21
Chap	22
You're a Dead Man Walking	24
Bard	26
Damaged Book	30
Critical Hour	32
The High-Line	34
Terminal Crossover	35
Automatic	37
The Shooting	39
Rothko Confession	42
Wavelength	44
Reverse Echo	46

A Stereo Shift

Charlie sits at a round table in a station café and looks across the room towards a table in the far corner where a lady repeatedly plunges a teabag in and out of the steaming hot water in her mug and the whole scene seems serene amongst the bustle of other customers coming and going and Charlie thinks that it might be alright to be lost in this moment forever and be in a perfect state of limbo and as you write this you know it is a load of bullshit and not because it hasn't happened but because Charlie is you and you are Charlie and you are already in hell and you know that it is too tragic to idealize and attempt to contain a fleeting moment and what you need to do is write about how you feel and although this will lead you into a dark place that you do not want to go to it will force you to deal with yourself from the outside in and you will feel pain and you will feel hatred for yourself and it is this very hatred that has consumed your mind for the last couple of years and it is a kind of hatred that you cannot turn outward on the world and as you come face to face with yourself and you put your experiences down on paper maybe you will be able to figure out a way to keep yourself alive.

Static Surround

You sit on the edge of the sofa holding a copy of Dostoyevsky's *The Gambler, Bobok, and A Nasty Story* while Danny packs his bag and you say to Danny:

"I've only read *The Gambler*.".

Danny looks up and says:

"Same."

You look at your watch and you have a sinking feeling in your chest because you are planning to commit suicide within the next few days and now it is time to drive Danny to the station and he is your closest friend and you are not ready to say goodbye and as you contemplate this painful situation you hand Danny the book and tell him:

"We need to think about going."

Danny slides the book into the front pocket of his bag and you stand up and open the front door and look out at the rain and then you head to your gun-metal grey VW Golf in the car park behind the house and you bring the car around to the front where Danny is now sheltering in the doorway and as you pull up Danny closes the house and walks down the path through the rain and he opens the passenger door and says:

"The rain sounds like static."

You start to say:

"I'm holding out for..."

You hesitate and continue:

"I don't know what I'm holding out for."

Danny climbs into the car and looks across at you and asks:

"You okay?"

You don't know what you can say because you are trying to hide the truth about the state you are in and stop yourself from spilling out at the seams and telling Danny what is going through your mind but you know that you need to keep on track with your plan to kill yourself and so all you can do is lie:

"I'm okay."

Slow Drift

You are in the station café talking to Danny and you wish time would slow down so you can spend some more time shooting the breeze and put off having to end your life and as you look across the cafe at the other customers Danny asks:

"You clocked the lady with the teabag?"

"Yes. I wondered if you'd clocked her as well."

Danny nods as he stands up and pulls on his coat and checks the time on his watch:

"I'd better head out to the platform. The train is due any minute."

You finish your espresso and Danny opens his bag and takes out a pocket notebook and three biro pens and hands them to you and you struggle to keep it together and Danny says:

"The pens are from the Ritz in Berlin."

All you can manage to say is:

"Perfect. Thank you. I'm glad you came to stay for a few days."

Your heart feels heavy as you pull yourself out of your seat and Danny starts to say:

"Please send my love to..."

You cut him off and say:

"Of course, I will."

And despite your answer you know it's too late to pass on his kind words because you don't intend to speak to her again and you plan to be dead before she returns from her business trip and then without giving the matter another thought you hold out your hand to shake Danny's hand and then he heads out onto the platform and boards the train and in your heart you believe this will be the last time you see him and before long the train disappears from sight and for the last few months you have been on a slow drift towards suicide but from this point forward you are in free-fall and your body begins to shudder and you run out of the station into the car park where you compose yourself and wipe away the tears on the cuffs of your coat and then you cross the asphalt to your car and you climb in and start the engine and as you pull out of the car park you look back at the station and beyond in the direction

Danny is travelling and you feel more alone and dislocated from the world than you have ever felt in your life.

Limits of Control

You park the car on the side of a road that runs through an industrial landscape and you get out of the car and lean on the open door resting on folded arms and you look at the bleak architecture and think about your circumstances and you try to work out when the coercion began but you can't pinpoint a specific moment in time and you suspect that the influence on you was subtle at first and then over a period of two years the increasing force of this negative influence resulted in you losing contact with friends and family and somehow at every step of the way you were compliant in shutting down those connections with the people that meant something to you and you don't know how you can ever reconcile yourself with this fact or even comprehend how you let this happen and aside from this for some reason your friendship with Danny has been permitted and there is no way to understand the sick strategy at play and yet there is some comfort to take from this because being allowed contact with Danny has meant that you have been able to break your last tie to the world on your own terms.

On the Sofa

You lie on the sofa fully dressed including your winter coat and navy Converse and your mobile phone starts ringing and you look across at the phone where it lies on the floor on a beige rug with a design of duck egg blue hoops and after a while the phone falls silent and you sit up and look around the room and the curtains are closed with the room only lit by the light from the hall and you think about how you have kept the room and the rest of the house immaculate and it is sparse with only an open notebook and a handful of pens spread across the dining table disturbing the effect of the décor that isn't minimal but tragically out of date and the phone starts ringing again and you mutter:

"Why don't you ring all the time?"

And you stand up and walk through to the hall and on into the kitchen where the décor is as dreary as the sitting room and you take a glass from the cupboard and fill it with water from the tap and you take a sip of water and pour the rest down the sink and then you wash the glass and carefully dry it before placing it back in the cupboard and you look out onto the street where the asphalt is starting to dry out following this morning's rain and then you return to the cupboard and take out the glass you used before and rewash it and dry it again and you make sure when you put it back on the shelf that it is neatly lined up with the other glasses in the cupboard and then the phone starts ringing again and while it rings you look at the calendar next to the fridge and check the date on your watch:

18th October.

21st October is marked on the calendar:

"JA RETURN."

You feel sick at the thought of her return and say to yourself:

"You have three days to end your life."

The phone buzzes and your stomach churns as you walk back into the sitting room and you pick up the phone from the beige rug with the out of date duck egg blue hoops and read the message:

"I tried to phone you but you didn't pick up. My trip has been shortened and I will be back tomorrow evening."

You cover your eyes and take a deep breath before throwing the phone into the corner of the sofa.

Cutback

The phone buzzes for the second time this morning and you stop making notes and push your notebook to one side and walk over to the sofa where you threw the phone earlier and you pick it up and even though the thought of what might be written in the message is terrible you open it anyway and read:

"When you clean the sheets, they need to be ironed before they go back on the bed. Wash and iron the towels that you use as well."

You walk upstairs and along the landing into the bedroom where you look at the bed which you haven't slept in and you take off your coat and place it on the floor and then you remove your shirt and t-shirt and look at the outside of your left arm which is streaked with cuts and scars and some are more violent than others and you look at your reflection in the mirror and you take a pen-knife out of your pocket and carry on carving lines into your arm and this is a slow and painful process but it is also empowering and when you stop cutting into your skin you look again at yourself in the mirror and you feel embarrassed and ashamed because of the desperation of this act of self-harm and then you take off your shoes and strip naked and you walk into the bathroom and turn on the shower and you let the water run on the back of your neck and then you was yourself and before long the bathroom fills with steam so you turn off the water and open the window and you sit down on the floor of the shower while the water drips off your body and you start to shiver but you hold out and don't give in to using one of the pristine towels and instead you stand up and attempt to wipe the last of the water from your body with your hands and you think:

"This is insane. Why am I punishing myself?"

Almost dry you step out of the shower and walk downstairs to the kitchen and gather cleaning materials from the cupboard under the sink and you head back upstairs to the bathroom and start cleaning and while you are scrubbing the shower it occurs to you to pour some bleach into the wounds on your arm and you do this because you feel compelled to suffer even though the pain is unbearable and after the pain eases you continue to clean the bathroom as if you were cleaning up a crime scene and when you have finished cleaning your mind is still a mess.

Normalization/ Dehumanization

In the bedroom you pull on a pair of jeans and a white t-shirt and your Converse and you take a black shirt from the cupboard that is creased with no evidence of ever having been ironed and that's how you like your shirts partly because wearing a creased shirt seems like an act of subversive defiance in an environment where at the very least you must resemble a normal human and behave like a normal human carrying out normal day to day activities like ironing your shirts and polishing your shoes and having normal conversations with people where you hold back from talking about either Gide or Bukowski to people who can't cope with existentialism and any impression of yourself that you create that is out of the ordinary is considered unsatisfactory and as you have been ground down to an idea of normality you have become alienated from yourself and invalidated as an individual and as this train of thought starts to eat up your mind you tell yourself to let it go and you find some calm and remember that you were about to pull on a creased shirt.

In the Glasshouse

You can't bring yourself to sleep in the bedroom anymore and although the sofa has been a temporary safe space it is no less a part of the psychological prison you are locked in and you pick up your coat from the floor and walk downstairs and you look at the sofa and see the impression that your head has left on the arm rest from sleeping on it the last few nights and also from when you have been lying on the sofa during the daytime and you try to smooth over the impression and this doesn't seem to help and you consider the magnitude of this issue and what it would mean for you if you were sticking around but thankfully you are bowing out of the game so it's no big deal and you don't need to give it another thought and you open the curtains and the patio doors and walk down the garden path to the shed and in the shed you find some cord amongst your belongings in a single box marked Charlie and while you walk back to the house you try to figure out how to tie a noose.

Hang Ten

You are standing in the loft looking down through the hatch at the stool lying on the ground that you kicked away as you hauled yourself up into the roof space and then you look up at the beams with a length of cord in your hand and you throw one end of the cord over one of the beams and tie it so that the cord is suspended over the hatch and you put your weight on it and it seems that the cord and the beam can take your weight and so you attempt to tie a noose but it's not right and it doesn't hold and you try again and you still can't get it right so you tie a simple hoop and slip it over your head and around your neck and you whisper:

"This is it."

And you move towards the edge of the hatch and you look down through the gap to the landing and you feel ready to jump and your eyes start to burn and you wipe away the tears and inch forward even further and then you hold off and remove the cord from your neck and slump down on the wooden boards not knowing whether to laugh or cry and you think:

"I can't even kill myself. I really am fucked."

From a London Bus

A few weeks ago you rode on the top deck of a London bus from Oxford Street to Whitechapel and you looked out of the window at the streets and the people walking to work and as the bus approached Russel Square you saw your father walking along the pavement smoking a Marlboro and you leapt out of your seat and you wanted to get off the bus immediately and talk to him and tell him how much of a mess you were in and you knew he would have held you and talked some sense into you and in a heartbeat he would have dropped everything to help you out but you were ashamed of your failures and also ashamed of the deterioration of your appearance and so you sat back down in your seat because you couldn't face your father seeing you like this and you slid further down in your seat out of sight from the street and felt a sharp pain of sadness in your throat and you broke your own heart in that instant.

Broken Record

The glass you drank out of earlier is playing on your mind and you wonder if you have washed it well enough and you can hear her words in your thoughts:

"Not good enough."

And these three simple words turn over and over and you feel pressure build up in your body and you walk into the kitchen and take the glass from the cupboard and smash it in the sink and you grind it into small shards with the palm of your hand and then there is blood and broken glass in the sink and you look at your hand and looking at the injury gives you some psychological relief and the unkind noise in your mind retreats and the pressure in your body subsides and you look out onto the cul-de-sac and say quietly:

"Shit. I'm going to have to clean this up."

Chap

You look out through the kitchen window and the street is empty and you try to leave the house as quietly as you can and you walk away from the house at pace and then you hear the front door of one of the neighbouring houses slam shut and you keep walking without looking over your shoulder but you hear a voice call out behind you:

"You alright chap?"

You stop walking and turn around to face the bulldog of a man and you say:

"Hello Alec. Are you well?"

"All good chap. Off out?"

"I'm heading out to get a takeaway."

Alec looks deep into your eyes and you start to get the sense that he is reading deep into your soul and you feel uncomfortable and you wonder if he can see that you are hollow inside and he says:

"Okay."

And he keeps looking into your eyes and you have to break his stare and so you make a move to walk off and he persists in conversation:

"How's the missus?" Haven't see her in a while."

You falter in your steps and smile and then answer:

"She is away on business. She will be back tomorrow. See you."

Sam crosses the road and Alec calls out:

"Alright. See you chap."

You're a Dead Man Walking

It takes you ten minutes to walk through the suburban maze of the estate and the walk takes you along empty streets and quiet alleyways and you keep your head down with your line of vision focused on your navy Converse and you are thinking you are better off dead and you make your way to the arcade of shops where the Chinese takeaway is and when you arrive you study the menu behind the glass window and then you enter and order some spring rolls and the man behind the counter gives you a number and you take a seat while the food is prepared in the busy kitchen and you wait for the number to be called and to your surprise the number is called quickly and you take the food and leave the takeaway and outside you sit on the curb between two parked cars and eat and once you have eaten you throw the rubbish in a nearby bin and look across the car park feeling lost and you can't face going back to the mausoleum of a house that you live in so you call for a taxi to drive you into the city and while you wait for the taxi you look up and imagine yourself hanging from a streetlight with a rope around your neck and this image in your mind isn't a big deal because your mind has been hijacked by projections like this and other similar scenarios for long enough now that you are accustomed to seeing yourself as dead and you compute the possibility that you are no more than a dead ringer for your future self.

Bard

The taxi drops you off in the city centre and you follow along sections of the old wall that line the city looking for a quiet place to have a drink and you look at your watch and the time is nine thirty and you come across the Albion Inn and you head into the entrance and take a door leading to the left of the bar and the room is dimly lit and filled with a somber air and aside from yourself there is an old couple playing cards with whiskies and three men drinking pints of ale and you walk up to the bar and the barman asks:

"What can I get you?"

You look at what is available and answer:

"A pint of Budweiser please."

And the barman pulls the pint and places the glass in front of you and you hand the man a ten-pound note and he rings it up on the till and passes you your change and you thank him and you walk over to a table that is in the window and you sit there with your drink studying the handful of people in the room and you drink the beer quickly and approach the bar for another beer and you also order a double house whiskey and head back to your seat and feeling a little relaxed you take your coat off and place it on the back of your chair and the door to the pub suddenly opens and in walks a large figure in a long coat wearing round glasses with black rims and he carries a briefcase and as he whisks into the room he brings in some of the cold air and you notice the man has white hair that is thin and parted to the side and you imagine he is a classics teacher and you take a sip of beer as this man looks around the room and greets the other patrons including yourself with a nod and he takes a seat on one of the bar stools which creaks as he shifts his weight to get comfortable and you observe the man with curiosity as he cradles a five-pound note in his hand and orders a drink:

"Please can I have a pint of the guest beer?"

The man swings round on his seat and faces you and starts to say:

"Up there."

The man points up above the bar and continues:

"Used to a hang a model of a ship? It was said to be cursed."

"Oh really?"

The barman places the beer ahead of the man and takes the five-pound note as the man carries on with his story:

"It is true. As the story goes, anyone who tried to move the ship would be cursed and they would drop down dead in the very place they were standing."

He looks up at where the model supposedly hung and you mutter under your breath:

"If only."

"What was that?"

You correct yourself:

"Quite a story."

The barman places the man's change on the bar and the man tells you:

"The ship would be as old as this pub. No one knows the ship's true provenance, but this pub has been here many years and has changed hands many times. The ship was right there the last time I had a drink in this pub. But that was fifteen or so years ago. I am surprised it has gone.'

The man picks up his beer and holds it up to you:

"Cheers."

You raise your glass and the man asks you:

"You're not from these parts, are you?"

You finish the last of your beer and answer:

"No."

You drink down the whiskey and walk up to the bar with the empty glasses and place them on the bar and you wish the man a good evening as you pull on your coat and you head out into the street and feel lost in the world.

Damaged Book

You open the front door and walk into the kitchen where you splash cold water onto your face to ease the effect of the alcohol and then you head into the sitting room and switch on a lamp in the corner behind the sofa and you walk over to a dresser behind the dining table under the stairs and you pull out a drawer where you keep a copy of Brautigan's *Tokyo Montana Express* amongst a handful of your possessions and you take out the old hardback copy and hold it in your hands and you close your eyes as you run your fingers down the spine and you feel where it is damaged and you have a flashback to a night sometime before when you had left the house to get some fresh air and escape the vile words that were being hurled at you and although you felt that you probably deserved the abuse it was too much to stand and her words still ring in your ears:

"That's right. Walk away like a weak, pathetic man."

Recalling those words fills you with shame and you remember that it wasn't weakness that drove you into the night but fear of the anger that was building up inside of you and once you were out of sight of the house you took out a pen-knife and sliced your arm until warmth ran up through your body and a sense of calm washed over you and the anger drained away and when you returned to the house later that night you found your copy of *Tokyo Montana Express* and your notebooks and pens thrown on the floor

Critical Hour

You are stretched out on the sofa again unable to sleep and you lie there and you are still fully dressed in your coat and trainers and you look up at the ceiling and then you check the time:

3 a.m.

You have passed a critical hour of the night when it is too late too to fall asleep and too early to be awake and so you pick up your copy of Brautigan's *Tokyo Montana Express* from the floor where you put it for comfort and you flick through the pages of the damaged 1980 edition and a piece of orange paper falls out onto your chest and you lower the book and look at the piece of paper that may have been used as a bookmark by a previous owner and you can see that it is an appointment reminder from over forty years ago:

Marion County Health Department
Family Planning Program
588-5355
Joan Wilson
Your appointment is scheduled for:
Date – 1/20/81

Time – 5.30 p.m.

Although you have looked at this piece of paper many times before it is only now that you place great value on this private biographical artefact that has come to be in your possession and you handle it with care and reading it makes you feel sad because you recognize its indescribable beauty and the emotional charge that it beholds and you can see that you have become used to trivializing life in the pursuit of destroying your own but that is the path you are on and you don't believe you can change this fact and so you slide the piece of paper back between the pages of the book and think about how you are going to terminate your own life.

The High-Line

You sit up on the sofa and switch on the television and you tune it to a sports channel and let the NASCAR highlights play in the background to counter the terrible silence in the house and you walk over to the dining table and sit down with a blank piece of paper and try to compose a suicide note and you can't figure out what to say and you write down some words and then you tear up the piece of paper because the words are sincere and hurtful and that seems unfair and you try and think of a way to sum up the reasons you are on this path and then you give up because your fall has been long and drawn out and now the conclusion is in sight it is difficult to focus on anything else and then your concentration drifts as you watch a red Chevrolet race round the circuit on the television and after a few minutes of watching the racing you write on a fresh piece of paper:

"I'm sorry I left an impression on the armrest of the sofa."

Terminal Crossover

You don't want to die here because this house has never felt like a home and you realize that you want to get as far away as possible and head to a place that means something to you and you decide to drive to Cornwall where you can swim out to sea and put everything behind you and it makes sense because you have a love for Cornwall from the times you have spent there while growing up and you think that in another life you might write about those times and without hesitation you pick up your notebook and pens and leave the house and head under the arch to the car park behind the houses in the cup-de-sac and you climb into your car and start the engine and you look at the steering wheel while thinking through your plan and then you reverse out of the space and drive out onto the street and you park up and you're about to take one last look at the house and you think better of it and pull away without looking back and that feels good and the estate becomes a blur and you turn out onto the main road and coast into a petrol station and fill up with fuel to see you through to your final destination and once you have paid for the fuel you leave the petrol station and trawl down to the motorway where you accelerate into the long drive south.

Automatic

It has taken you six and a half hours to drive to St. Ives and now you are here you know that you can be at peace with yourself as you live out the last few hours of your life and you lean on the bonnet of the car as you look out across the sea and you reflect that as a point of departure Porthmeor Beach is a good choice and you feel pretty calm about the fact that in a few hours you will swim out to sea and you step forward from the car and walk over to the ticket meter and buy a parking ticket and you imagine that these machines are on borrowed time and at some point in the near future they will be obsolete and replaced by a fully automated digital payment system and you decide to head into the town centre and you leave the car park and walk down the hill and from Barnawoon you cut along Barnoon Terrace and then you head down Academy Place descending the steep set of stone steps to Fore Street and as you turn onto Fore Street you enter the crowd of tourists and locals and stop to re-tie a shoelace and while you tie your shoelace a stretch of empty space opens up ahead and you remember a line from Apollonius's *Argonautica*:

'Turn back a little space in the sea.'

The crowd stacks up behind you and a man knocks your shoulder with his beach bag putting you a little off balance and the man looks down at you with a scowl and other people filter past and fill the space in front of where you are kneeling and you become submerged in a sea of people and you stand up and pull your t-shirt forward from your neck and you look for the man with the beach bag and you wonder if you should have it out with him but you can't see him for all the people and instead you navigate across the drift of the crowd and you turn onto Court Cocking and follow the spiralling alleyway down to the harbour.

The Shooting

You are in the amusement arcade overlooking the harbour and you pick up a rifle in the shooting alley and look down the sight and focus on a target and you shoot and miss and you aim for another target and this time you hit the bullseye and this causes a jet of water to shoot out at the people standing to your side and you apologize and you put down the rifle and strange memories from your childhood resurface as hazy images of burnt out and turned over cars swim through your thoughts and you are back in 1985 when you were six and you were travelling with your parents back to England, from Fuschl in Austria at the end of a family holiday and the drive took you through Bavaria and on past Munich and once past the border into Belgium your father picked up the pace and you sensed your mother was anxious and then your father slowed on the entrance to a village and you could see a group of boys a few years older than yourself standing on a grass verge in front of a building and one of the boys raised an air rifle and pointed it directly at the car and you heard a loud crack against the windscreen and in front of your father an indentation with small lines stretching out in three directions formed on the glass in an instant and you looked out at the boys peering after the car and the boy with the rifle was now holding the weapon by his side and you looked back at your father as he carried on driving and your mother asked him:

"What was that?"

And without hesitation he answered:

"A stone flicked up from the road and chipped the windscreen."

You didn't contradict him and you tried to look again at the boys but they were now far behind and you didn't understand at the time why the boy shot at the car but later in life you would come to learn that this was the morning following the Heysel Stadium Disaster where a fight led by English fans broke out and resulted in people being caught between the crowds and a crumbling wall and many people died as a result of the riots before the start of the UEFA Final between Liverpool and Juventus in Brussels and because of this cars with English number plates were an easy target and for the rest of the journey you held tight onto the seat belt in the back of the white Ford Escort XR3I as your father raced for the ferry at Ostend and then your thoughts return to the present in the shooting alley and you want to call your parents and tell them that you miss them but you know you can't because hearing their kind voices might derail you from your plan to kill yourself.

Rothko Confession

You want to look at some paintings before you die and you head to Tate St. Ives following the road up from the harbour to Back Road West under a cerulean sky and you cross the asphalt at the corner of the street where Back Road West turns into Digey Flats and as you come out of the shade you hold up your notebook to shield your eyes from the sun and a half-eaten Cornish pasty lies on the cobble stones that lead up to The Digey and a restored Volkswagen beach buggy trawls down Back Road West and the nose of the beach buggy twitches as the driver brakes into the corner before heading down Digey Flats and the thunder of the air-cooled Beetle engine echoes amongst the buildings and everyone around stops to gaze at this beast before it disappears from sight and you notice a seagull dart forward and drag away the pasty with its beak and you continue on towards Tate St. Ives and you go into the museum and walk around the galleries and while you look at Rothko's *Untitled 1950-2* you find yourself alone in the gallery and you step forward and run your hand gently over a section of Rothko's painting and you are blown away by the delicacy of the paint on the canvas and the beauty of the surface seems distant from the macho image of the group of New York abstract expressionists that Rothko was a part of and you stand back from the canvas upon which you have left a trace of yourself and you recall a time before when you looked at this painting in 1996 and you listened to the gallery assistant explain that in 1970 he had been in London unpacking Rothko's *Seagram Murals* to be hung close to Turner's paintings at the Tate Gallery when the team at the gallery received a fax from New York to let them know Rothko had committed suicide.

Wavelength

You walk back in the direction of the car park and consider driving back north where you can pretend to be normal and not about to self-destruct and you stop at the car and look at your reflection in the glass and you don't like the person you see and you decide not to get in and you carry on to the corner of the car park and open a gate leading into Barnoon Cemetery and you close the gate behind yourself and the constant rush of the sea rumbles as the water rolls in and pulls out from Porthmeor Beach and you walk over to Alfred Wallace's grave overlooking the coastline and you look at the tiles that were fired by Bernard Leach and then you kneel down and touch the grave with your hand and you close your eyes and take a deep breath before standing up again and then you head down through the graveyard to the foot of Porthmeor Hill and as you step out onto the road you push back your hair from your face and you walk down the stone steps below Porthmeor Beach Café to the sand and you keep walking until you are at the water's edge and you look up at the sky and shout:

"I'm ready."

And you start walking out into the sea and your phone starts ringing and you stop and the water comes up to your knees and you take the phone out of your pocket and you answer it and you hear at the other end of the line:

"Charlie. Where are you? It sounds like you are by the..."

You hang up the phone and throw it like a skimming stone across the surface of the water and without bouncing the phone just disappears into the crest of a wave and you smile and take a few more steps further out until you are waste deep in the sea and you ask yourself:

"What the hell are you thinking?"

You look out into the distance at the horizon and by chance you remember sitting in a cafe across from a lady as she repeatedly plunges a teabag into her mug of hot water and this small detail of a memory breaks your resolve and you concede that you have a connection with the world and that you are not ready to leave just yet and so you walk back up to the beach where you sit down on the sand and feel good to be alive.

Reverse Echo

You were.

He is.

I will be.

Born in 1979, Flemming George currently lives in Oxfordshire with his wife and two children. He was shortlisted for the Bath Novella in Flash Award 2024. He has had stories included in anthologies published by Pure Slush and Truth Serum Press and his story, Modulated Transition was included in Dandelion Years: Bath Flash Fiction Volume Seven. He studied fine art at University of Oxford and drawing at University of the Arts London.

Printed in Great Britain
by Amazon